When The Blackbird Whistles
The Tales of Tralia
Book One

Anita K. Mills

When The Blackbird Whistles

The Tales of Tralia

Book One

Published by Blakeman Books

First Printing, 2022

Blakeman Books
Anita Blakeman-Mills
4 Morton Avenue
Ilkeston Derbyshire DE7 8WD
https://blakemanbooks.weebly.com

DEDICATION

To my sister, Paula, for always being there.

To my Daughter, Diane, for all her hard work over the past years, including her help and companionship.

To my family for their patience in listening to me as I read out the next chapter.

Table of Contents

Foreword
One: The Letter
Two: Hakorn
Three: Old Wounds Closed
Four: A Diversion
Five: A Disused Fear
Epilogue
Characters
From the Author
Other Books

Disclaimer

Any references to historical events, real people or real places are used fictitiously. Names, characters and places are products of the author's imagination.

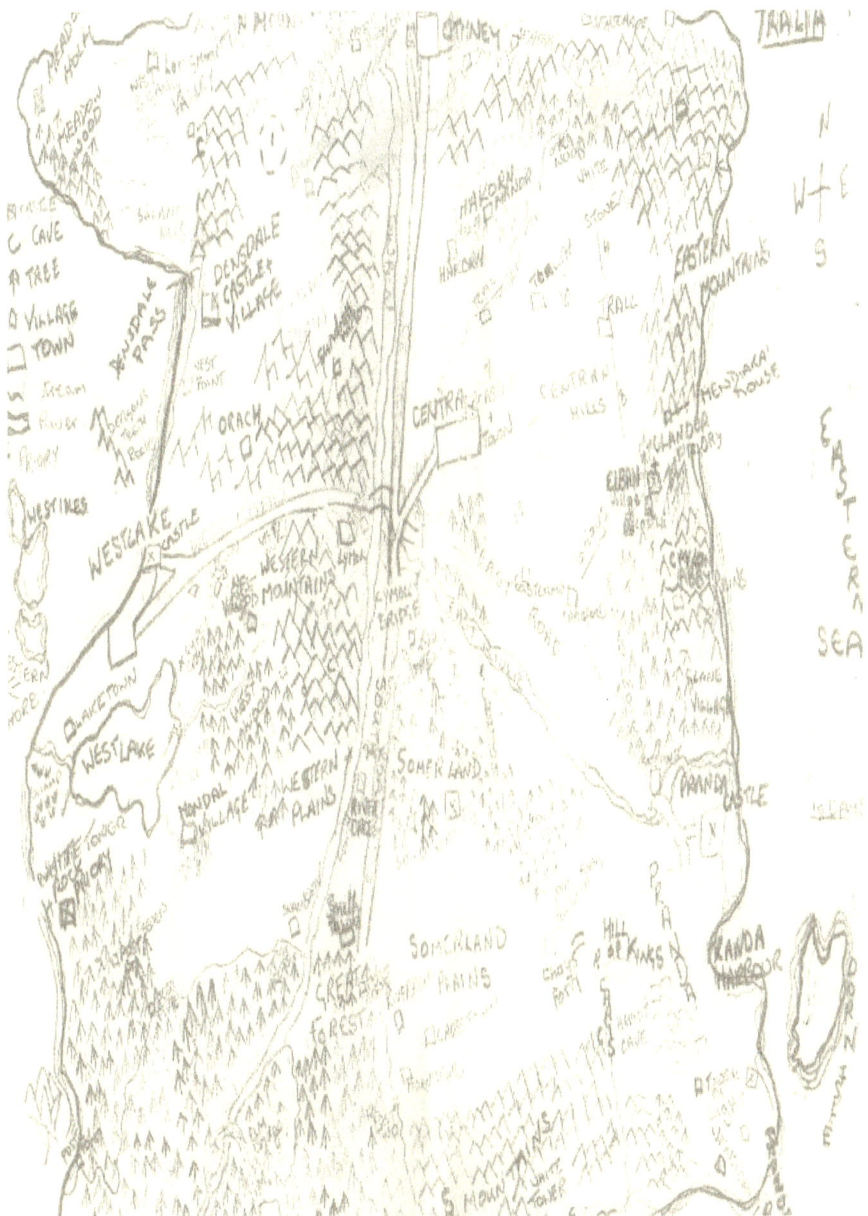

MAP OF TRALIA

FOREWORD

I finally slipped off my shoes and placed them beside the couch before putting my feet up. What an exhausting day to be sure. But my prime was finally alone with his wife and I, Gregor, First Minister of Pranda, could now go to bed.

Tomorrow I am away to the Prandain Hills as I am going to see a man about a boat. I have already seen the sailboat in the harbour, now I have tracked down the owner, who lives in Chaysford, to offer him a fair price. I have no wife to worry about as the only woman I ever cared anything for decided that this life was too rich for her and married a fisherman many years ago. So, it's just me and my dog, Clem. I had the animal from a pup, but like me, he was now a bit long in the tooth and walking was about all the poor thing could do now and even that is an effort, hence the boat. I planned to spend my retirement days at sea or on the river. Either way, I could not wait for it to begin. When an adventure comes knocking in the early hours of the morning, but I have already had one adventure too many, so what will this adventure cost me, as I cannot refuse?

The Mission

I have been given a mission to find The Blackbird. To find Philip Hakorn, the leader of the Blackbird warrior guild, who was taken from his home. Riding around Tralia looking for answers that could cost me my life was not my first choice once released from my duty. I have just retired as the first Minister of Pranda and was looking forward to my retirement, as I am too old to go gallivanting around Tralia. My hunting, climbing, horse racing days are well and truly behind me. But this search leads me from my old training ground, down to the southern forest and into one of the river towns that holds more secrets than I thought possible, but we must find my friend at all cost. There was more to this than an abduction, I was sure. What did Philip know that he became a target?

The Blackbird warriors were all summoned and when The Blackbird whistles all listen and obey.

Chapter One
The Letter

I groaned as the bell chimed two. The annoying sound awoke me, and I got up slowly. Sleeping on the hard bench couch was not good at my age, so I dragged my sorry self into the bedroom and lay down on the bed. Clem had followed me and lay on his near the window. He never even looked up and, like me, was asleep the moment his head touched the pillow. I pulled the thick quilted blanket up over my shoulders and dreamed, the dream I had for many a-night, going back almost forty years.

Her tall, silhouette figure stood close, but not touching me. Her face was in shadow, too dark to make out, but I knew by my heart who it was.

My sleeping form turned, but my dreaming self-opened my eyes a little as I growled. She was so far out of my reach that I could not touch her, yet I could breathe in her scent that was so intoxicating. I wanted more, more than anything else in the world.

She banged her foot hard on the wooden floor. 'Don't!' She said through gritted teeth in an angry whisper. 'I'm not yours. Stop calling me here. Please leave me be.'

I cannot, I thought. *I miss you.* My heart spoke back.

The bang came again as she faded further in the shadows. 'I know, but I belong to another.' Her words hung in the air.

Another bang, but it wasn't Kiela. Disturbed, I opened my eyes fully and blinked hard, then rubbed the sleep out of them. Clem was already moving to the door, wagging his tail. Slowly, I moved too, groaning before sitting up. There it was again; someone was definitely banging. The noise echoed through to the bedroom. Who could it be at this hour? *Dawn can't be far off*, I thought tiredly, and it was too early for the boaters. It could be

Sandras! I stumbled off the bed after pushing the cover aside. I opened the bedroom door and headed out into the hall. Clem padded off towards the main door as soon as I got there. My rooms in the castle were in the east wing, facing the boat yard. I didn't have to worry about the noise because I was up at dawn, before they started work and I did not get to bed till late, after the boaters had gone home.

I reached and opened the front door. There stood Quickfeet, who held out a hand with a missive. He petted Clem with his other as I took it. "Sorry," he mumbled, "thought you would be awake."

Luckily, I was still dressed, so I pulled out my change purse and gave the three coins required. Well, the boy had run up two flights of stairs, so he deserved it. I thanked him and closed the door. Who could it be? I stopped as I turned the letter over and saw the stamp on the red wax. I groaned again, but deeper this time. This, I knew, wasn't good.

The silhouette of a caged blackbird was deeply ingrained into the wax and as I broke the seal across the neck, my fingers shook. It had been thirty-five years since I'd seen the symbol of the warrior creed in a letter, other than on my hand. I wondered what they wanted from me now, an old man, whose hunting, climbing, horse racing days were well and truly behind him and I have had one adventure I didn't care to repeat.

I had been the chosen king's guardian right from an early age and had trained hard to rise high and at twenty-five they had given me the watch of the then heir to Pranda. Though they raised the heir to be king, it was not to be. Not long after we had escaped from the Sorcerer's Daughter, over forty years ago, the five heirs decided on one heir and four primes. I did not care who ruled the country. I was just glad my prince, and I were home safe. Then the prince had done something really stupid and made me his first minister.

But for ten years, I had served two masters. I had continued my warrior training and watched over my friend, but as I got older, I knew I couldn't be faithful to the two. So, I had to bow out of the warrior guild and get sworn in to the ministerial position, which I have hated all my life. But because Sandras and I had become good friends, I could not turn him down when the old first minister died, leaving no heir.

My heir had been my brother-in-law. I sneered, knowing the man liked the lifestyle he had become used to when he married Isabel, my sister. Yet, he had done hardly any work to earn the position and wasn't really First Minister material. I hadn't liked the man from the moment my sister introduced him to the family, but our father took a liking to him and they made plans for a wedding. Luckily for me, I had no son. So, I could choose who I wanted to follow me and after my brother-in-law's death a few years ago, my nephew, my sister's only child, became my heir. With one son and three daughters to marry off well, the man needed a well-paid job. Once away from his father's eye, he became rather a good political advisor. He was also good with a blade and had stood up to the training at Hakorn and had worked hard by my side for the past ten years and was now ready to take my place as first minister.

My Prime Sandras could take care of himself, so I had no problem leaving my nephew in charge of the first minister's office, now I had retired. My nephew had married well, I had seen to that. After his father died, he had taken in his mother to watch over her. My influence had paid off.

I could reminisce all I wanted but could not put off reading the letter any longer, so I opened it up and read the words quietly to myself.

My friend, even after all these years, I still know where to find you, at your prince's side. You have served him well, but now the guild needs your expertise. I need your help, as someone has threatened us from the inside.

Someone is trying to destroy not only our guild, but all the guilds. Even the magic one.

What, I thought, *all fourteen*? I shook my head. I did not want to go traipsing over the country at my age, but when the blackbird whistles, you answer.

'Please come and help me. I need you, old friend. We all do!'

It was unsigned, but I didn't need a signature. Only Phillip of Hakorn Manor, The Blackbird, the leader of the warrior guild could have sent this, and I knew I had to go, but I did not like it and I wasn't going alone!

I stripped, washed, and found my travel bag before I dressed in the traditional black. I placed my Prandain armband over my coat's right sleeve, then filled my bag with necessities before putting on my boots. Clem looked up miserably as I picked up my bedroll, which had been cleaned recently from the closet. Did the Goddess know? I walked out of the bedroom, followed by Clem with his head and tail down.

It was almost dawn as I heard Prandain's Chapel bells ring out the time as I stopped in the hall. There, neatly placed were the parchments and pens on the side bench, and I jotted two missives. Though I wrote a cheery note to Sandras, he would pick up the underlying words telling the prime where I was going. I had no secrets from my friend and had even taught him a trick or two in case he needed it. He, in turn, taught his two sons and then sent them to Hakorn.

The five high minsters set it up when Tralia was threatened and their princes taken sixty years ago. They trained certain prominent sons so that never again could an enemy take an heir. Boy, did they fail when Sandras, heir to the then Prandain throne, was taken prisoner alongside his body guard. Though he wasn't the target; the Sorceress of Tralia's children were.

Tilda, the Sorcerer's daughter, had captured them, but we were all caught up in the woman's evil scheme to restore her crazy father's mind with some staff from the first Tralian Sorcerer. But we escaped and then helped the Sorceress to destroy the Sorcerer's daughter and her mercenaries. Or so we thought. Three years later, they attacked Hakorn Manor and all but one died.

Phillip had become the first minister of Orthney and was away from home, or they might have killed him, too. After a year of mourning, he made the guild sit up and become a force to be reckoned with, by bringing a few Solenteers into their circle. Trained Monks from the watchtowers to teach prime and first Minister's heirs. Though swords were their chief weapon, they were all trained in many other things, including the staff and also stealth, and no heirs were taken again.

Philip could not save his brother-in-law when the Ambassador of Tralia was murdered, as he did not know who handled his brother-in-law's murder. I knew he blamed himself for not knowing, and it wasn't until Kathryn, the Sorceress, had found out who had killed her son and with the help of her adopted son Martin, she had been following Michael's trail and destroyed the last remaining heir to Medrith's madness a few seasons ago. There were a few hangings for sure, but what could Philip be referring to that I had the expertise to help? Expert in what?

I wrote a second message to my nephew wishing him good luck in his new job. Though he wouldn't need it, I had taught him well, and he had become better than I.

I went downstairs, listening to Clem's nails clicking on the stairs. As I entered the large hallway, I called a missive boy over. "Take this to the prime's room," I told him, "And give it only to the Prime. This other one…" I waved in front of his nose, "leave in the first minister's office."

I flipped him a silver coin and knew he would deliver my messages. I continued down the hall into the servant's quarters and hurried into the groom's hall. Only two were up at this time of day, and one quickly ran to saddle my horse. He took Clem, my bag and bedroll with him, while I spoke to the night chef. It wasn't long before I had a travel pack of food for a week and a couple of pasties to take with me, fresh from the oven. I walked out into the yard eating one. It was cold, as the sun was only just rising. I was grateful for my new cloak.

I climbed into the saddle and grasped Clem and we left by the south gate leading into the town. My first port of call was to my nephew's house and to find Conner, my great nephew, who at seventeen was a magnificent sword man and a Blackbird trainee, upon my suggestion and was home for a break. My horse clattered into the courtyard and I removed myself from the saddle. I was already aching, as it had been a while. As the boy ran, half-awake from the stable, I lowered the dog and place him on the ground. "Saddle Conner's horse and water mine." I instructed.

He nodded and disappeared back into his domain. I hurried to the side door, where Clem was waiting for me. I called into the kitchen and spoke to the cook. He nodded, and I left.

I found Conner's room up a flight of stairs and, luckily, found him dressing. Of course, he had heard me enter by the delivery entrance and my words with the boy below his window.

"Where to, uncle?" he asked without preamble.

I smiled. That's what I liked about the boy. Never asked stupid questions. "Hakorn," I replied as he petted Clem, "and I'll explain on the way, except to say I'm needed."

Again, I had said enough for him. Something must be up at the manor as the first minister only ever went to see his friend, not on Blackbird business. I saw his mind working. Nodding, the boy picked up his sword and travel bag. We left as quietly as I came. I dropped Clem off into the kitchen where he was made a fuss of and though he tried to follow, it was only a halfhearted attempt. As when I left on business, I always left him here with the staff. We picked up Conner's travel pack. Outside, after a brief word with the boy by Conner, telling him to tell his parents he was with me, Conner climbed into his saddle, while I re-seated myself. Soon, we were riding out of the city. Our way was north, first along the east road, then up across country behind the capital, Centra to the old river ford and then into Hakorn Valley. A seven-day journey. Some nights sleeping in taverns, others on the hard ground. Even though we were in the first throws of spring, winter still had a frozen grip. I pulled my cloak tighter around me.

Only when we made camp at dusk did I relay why I was going. Again, no stupid questions came out of my young companion's mouth, but he made a sharp one.

"Who could be behind this new threat?"

I could not answer, as I did not know. The country had only just settled down after the death of Michael, the Tralian Ambassador. The entire country had and still mourned the son of the Sorceress and there was still a lot of anger that had yet to dissipate.

Both my prime and I attended the funeral, but we had only spoken to Martin afterwards, as his adopted mother was in no fit state to speak to anyone and his adopted father had gone out asking questions, in and around town, trying to get answers. But apparently, none were forthcoming. We returned home and asked our own, but the killers were elusive until Kathryn began following her son's trail into and beyond the northern mountains to kill those responsible. Once back in Tralia, they hoped to catch up with Medrith's heir. Hopefully, that was the last of that crazy family.

We returned to work as the affairs of the city were mounting up.

Now something else was shaking up the affairs of Tralia and it seemed they needed me, though for what purpose I could not guess.

We talked during supper of the Ambassador's death. The king had informed the Primes of the travels of the Sorceress and then of the battle on the Northern Plains. Though we sent soldiers and the heir to Sandras, we ourselves were too old. But there was more than Medrith's son abroad during this time and the Sorceress was still looking. The Primes, too, were keeping a tight hold on the incoming and outgoing of their cities and towns. Even the elves were watching over the forest and mountain passes for any news of the renegade Sorcerer's army, but so far, no news had reached Pranda that it had regrouped, yet they must be somewhere!

"It's a shame," remarked Conner, "The Ambassador will be missed. He did much for Tralia and is it true, there is none to take the Sorceress' place when she dies?"

I nodded. "Aye, it's true. But let's hope that this blackbird business does not intrude into her chance to finally grieve?"

He nodded his agreement.

We slept till sunrise and began our second day of riding. The skies held a promise of rain, but the weather, though chilled, did not break into the threatening storm. We stopped at midday to rest the horses and, after feeding and watering the four of us, we began our journey once again.

Nothing changed until after the capital and we were on the north road. The threatened rain began and muddied our route. It was like a sheet, and within a bell, we nestled into a crag in the hills and settled back to wait for the weather to change.

"Any thoughts on what Master Philip needs you for?"

I shook my head as I looked out over the hills. We were climbing high into the northern territory and though the rain cut the view, sometimes I could see into the murky grey and a few hills beyond.

"He said someone threatened the guilds from inside and as there are fourteen guilds, this someone wants something."

He nodded. "From the inside. Hmmm. As I know all the masters, only one comes to mind who disagrees with Master Philip regularly and that is Master Greylan. But I cannot see him pulling a fast one. Though he's older than Phillip, he is a firm friend. Philip said the old master keeps them on their toes. Yet, I wonder if his grandsons are the ones? They cause trouble at every turn."

He began telling me of the masters, their teachings and their personal habits. In the two years the boy had taken my advice of 'to watch more than he learns,' it will help on the outside away from the school. He keeps to his studies well, and none of the masters have cause to complain about his work or his behaviour. As his benefactor, all reports come to me via Phillip's office. Though Phillip himself does not teach now, he still has the school to run. The school holds six First Minister's sons and the heir to the elvish throne, plus any who can afford the high fees that Phillip charges along with the prime heirs. There are also places for the 'exceptionally gifted' under nobles and even free-borne to attend on scholarships that are recommended by teachers from any school in Tralia. Also, recommendations come from the towers, though no magic born was allowed. They have their own schools and their own masters set up by the now dead ambassador. A great legacy and he was the one who suggested a revival and alterations of all the guilds. Yes, he would be missed.

The boy had told me of the students. Most were like himself; they study and behave. The two, he already mentioned, Jayson and Bradshaw, were brought to my attention on more than one occasion in Phillip's mail asking for advice on how to deal with them. I thought boredom might be the problem. Give them more studies and extra work, I advised, and for a while it seemed to work. They quieted down. But it seems they are back at disrupting the school again. Even their own grandfather cannot, it seems, rule them.

Phillip has given them one more chance or they are to leave.

Well, those two don't really fit the bill, unless disrupting the school is their aim, but who gives the orders?

I asked him, "Tell me more about the masters."

Master Chellin was the weapons master and retires to his room soon after supper. Master Corson was the political advisory teacher and liked a tipple, but alone. Then there was the math teacher, Master Brodel. A quiet man always agreed with Phillip. A yes man. Master Zarendrith, the Elfin stealth and hand-speak teacher and last, Master Markin, the rest of the curriculum teacher, Tralian geography and history. He was new to the school replaced the previous three-curriculum teacher after his death only a few years ago. So, there were fourteen students and five teachers, along with

Phillip and his clerk, Drevis, who replaced the murdered clerk of forty-one years ago, when tragedy struck. They murdered all in the village and in the manor. They only missed his sister because she had fallen asleep in the old tower. So, no one stood out, but then spies and disrupters never do. Instead, they whisper in ears.

"There doesn't seem to be a finger pointer in any of them?" I pointed out.

He agreed. "Then, except for the staff of the kitchen and the manor grounds, are we really looking for an inside man?"

"That's what Philip told me."

"So, Master Phillip holds more information?" He related softly just before the lightning struck, though some way off.

I agreed, wondering if the storm was about to pass overhead tonight or land on us. It landed two hours later, and we got a little sleep that night trying to hold up the tarpaulin. After a cold breakfast, we climbed back into the saddle.

We reached the old ford a day later and stocked with extra bread after a night's sleep, though they had little choice. Then, we left the town, hoping to make up at least half a day. But just on the outskirts, I noticed a shadow in the hills behind us. Which was strange as there was no sun.

I saw a movement out of the corner of my eye, a split moment after Conner, who moved his hand. Conner acknowledged my answer. We entered the trees that surrounded the large manor and set up camp, as we had one more night to go. However, instead of lying in camp, we took to the bushes behind the camp and laid in wait.

Just after dark, we heard at least three men trying stealthily to approach. Our poor packs were stuck more than once with the blades of two of the attackers. The third stood looking shocked at the viciousness the other two applied to their thrusts, but neither did they have time to be astonished as we stepped out of the bushes. The two who killed our packs stepped to meet us, but died within the first few moments. Conner was quicker than I. The other one put up a half-hearted fight and when we injured him, he gave up as he did not want to die like his companions, as he was only there for the food. Though it was only a scratch.

Asked to explain as his only offer to live was to tell us why and who hired them? To which he agreed, but the man I killed was the one who hired him, and he had said that I could not reach Hakorn. They did not say 'dead.' They did not tell him why or who hired them. With no magic user with us, I had to accept his answers, but why wasn't I wanted at Hakorn? This puzzled me, as I had only been an adviser for forty years. I did not live there and was never a master, unless I knew something? Something someone did not want me and Philip to discuss. Could it really have something to do with forty years ago? It was the only thing I could think of at the moment.

The man who said his name was Rylan of Orthney had only joined them a week ago and only because he was hungry.

I asked, "What work have you done before and who have you done work for?"

"I worked for Manshell. The leader of the merchant guild, who lives in Riverfalls." was his answer, "Well, at least until he died and with no heir, his lands were forfeit. It went to the crown. The new master brought his own staff with him, but because of my sword, they kept me on, until he, too, died a month later, again with no heir. So, I hired myself out and as I hadn't eaten in two days, I took this job. Shame about my old masters, them both dying a month apart and no heirs?"

I asked him to explain again.

"Manshell's son was an excellent rider yet fell off his horse and broke his neck, and there were no tracks to say they were racing. Then they found the master beside his horse with a broken neck too, near to where they found his son, and again the hooves suggested only walking. The coroner decided it was a misadventure. One maybe, and I disagree with that, but two? I did not think so, but could not say different."

"And who was your new master?" Conner asked.

"Lord Trayval, the Justice of the Peace for the northern territory. Then my new master died of a stroke even though he seemed healthy enough and he had just married. I left soon after, as I did not like the third."

"And the man who gained Trayval Hall?" I asked, recognising the name.

Lord Swaincoat of Riverfalls, I was told. Another name I recognised, and it seemed so did my companion. And I could not blame Rylan for not staying. That man had a poor reputation, at best.

Now what to do with the would-be assassin?

Chapter Two
Hakorn

We clattered through the two large metal gates onto the cobbled yard two days later. It was hard riding and with no more attempts on my life. Yet here something was amiss?

No one came out to greet us, so leaving the horses hitched to the post in the front yard, we entered the large manor by the front door. To the left were the family rooms and to the right was the new building of the school. Knowing Conner could take care of himself, he went right. While I went to find Phillip's office, Rylan took the stairs. Yet the house seemed empty.

I knew Nicholas, Philip's son, spent most of the time in the Castle at Orthney as first minister, along with his son, but Phillip lived here with his sister, Talaya, and their staff. His granddaughter now lived in Centra with her royal husband, yet room after room was empty, even of staff, but nothing was out of place. Curious, I went back into the hall just in time to meet Conner. He shook his head.

"No one," he whispered.

"Same." I stated in the same vein as Rylan came down the stairs. His find was negative, too. We went towards the backdoor to enter the backyard.

Just then, I heard a sound. Leather on stone. Like a boot thumping on the ground. Slowly, with swords drawn, I opened the kitchen door as quietly as I could. Outside on the hard-baked floor lay two old men and an old woman, bound and gagged. One man and the woman I recognized, they were the clerk and Phillip's sister. The other, an old man, was a stranger. As I bent to help the three on the ground, the other two looked around. They found the barn was full of the staff.

After we had untied them, we helped those that needed their beds. We treated shock as well as minor injuries, but luckily no fatalities. We sat in the family's sitting room and listened as an appalling tale was told. Conner made tea and, between Talaya Hakorn, and the clerk, Dervis, they told us what happened. The old man sat quietly, drinking his tea. His paler was not good. I believed him to be the old school Master, whom I had never met.

Two days after the students and their teachers had left for their vacations, men in black, at least ten, maybe a dozen of them rode in through the main gate.

"The poor gateman was killed, and they woke Philip before they took him prisoner and questioned him at length. They threatening harming us if he did not talk, but we did not hear what they wanted," said the clerk.

"They tied the rest up in the barn and guarded them. This morning they brought us out and threatened again if my brother did not ride with him." Added Talaya.

"Who were they?" asked Conner, handing her another cup of tea.

"That's just it," replied the clerk. "We don't know. Only one man spoke, and his accent was unusual. Late forties, dark eyes and he found Tralia difficult, and the rest spoke in a language I did not recognise. They all wore a snake around a pole tattoo. Again, I've never seen any of them before, but they headed south."

"How do you know that?" asked Conner suspiciously.

"Cus, I told them." Said a small voice from the doorway. A boy of around seven now stood in the room and was holding a sword, which was too heavy for him, but though his eyes were wide with fear and shock, he stood his ground for a moment or two. Then he dropped the sword and ran to the stranger, who had yet to speak.

"Grandfather, I'm sorry. I could not let them hurt you again."

"They will not. This is a Blackbird and he will find Master Philip, and all will be right again."

"But, grandfather, I disobeyed you!"

"Hush, child, you are safe. We are all safe now and by watching, you have set the Blackbirds on the path. Soon, the birds will fly home and Master Gregor will have help. You did well."

"I did?" The boy asked in awe with large wondrous eyes. "That's good then, but what of Jay and Brad?"

"They will get their comeuppance, Marcus." Said the old man. "I cannot, nor will I defend them ever again. Only the Goddess can save them now."

So, He knew who I was and two of Greylan's grandchildren were part of a kidnapping group.

"What did they do?" I asked.

"They killed the gateman and then let them in. They hit my grandfather. My cousins are not to be trusted and I will never forgive them," said Marcus, shaking his head.

"Do you remember anything else?" I asked, including the others in the question. Most shook their heads.

"I don't. They kept us away from the others as a threat to my brother. Yet they never asked us anything," replied Talaya. "It was strange. Apparently, only Philip was required." The other two nodded their heads in agreement.

"Were the boys here, or had they left and came back with them?"

"Here," said Greylan, "it seemed strange they were usually the first to go, but not this time. I did not find out till they walked in for breakfast yesterday."

"They had a map, they kept passing it back and forth to each other and grinning," put in Marcus. "I saw it, it. was of Tralia and had lots of dots on it."

"Are you sure, boy?" asked his grandfather. The boy nodded. He ran from the room and came back with a map.

"This is mine. All young fledglings get one to learn the land."

I nodded, remembering, but where my copy was now after all these years, I would be hard pressed to remember. He placed his on the table and, with a feather and a pot of ink, he began dotting places on the map. "I hope I get a new one. All these," he said, "were black, but Hakorn," he tapped the map. "There was a red circle. This one in Orthney had a cross through it. As well as this one in Centra and this one in Riverfalls, but this place had another circle around it. Rivertown, its down the south road. Fourteen dots, two circles and three crosses."

"What could it mean?" asked Talaya.

"Not known yet." I replied, not wishing to alarm her anymore as I remembered Rylan's story of his previous master and where he lived.

We searched the boys' rooms upstairs, but we found nothing. The doves went out to all known active blackbirds to watch out for Greylan's grandsons and to meet up at any of these nearest towns. The Blackbird was quiet. I put. We sent a copy of a list of towns and cities that the heads lived in and the Blackbirds of that place were to watch over the heads of guilds. They were to send word of any attempt on their lives. I was on my way to Riverfall and might need a hand. We set off south, following the abductor's trail.

Conner's eyes were better than mine, and he kept a close eye on the marks made by the hooves of the kidnappers, and so far, Rylan was proving his worth. He was a damn wonderful cook.

"I learned as I live alone," he said, "and I like to cook."

He was also a better swordsman than made out to be earlier, but then he wasn't into murder, he told us. I had a feeling I could trust him, but I needed to be sure.

Hakorn had filled our food bags up generously.

The tracks we followed, where not hidden, so Conner had no problem. *Did they know they were being followed or did they not care?* That thought, I could not shift. We stopped to feed ourselves and the horses. We camped from dusk and slept till dawn, but it still took four days before we entered Riverford. We timed our night arrival well after waiting in the trees nearby, till after dark.

The gatekeeper told us that a dozen men had ridden into town earlier that day, but not together. "One of the five men had a snake tattoo. When another group turned up a quarter bell later, I saw a second and knew they came from the same place, though I don't know where."

I moved closer and asked, "Where were they now or have they continued South or to a new place?"

"North and South," he replied. The first five went north, and the seven went south by boat, but shook his head. "They threatened a captain, but they had gone before the watch came. You'd best go to the Riversedge inn. That's a better place to sleep than the forest. Too many cutthroats in there nowadays."

I thanked him and slipped a coin. He was grateful, as was I. So they had separated, but I still think Rivertown was our best bet.

We set off at dawn the next morning after a quick breakfast at the inn. Conner quickly picked up their trail, but he could not tell whether five, ten, or twelve, as they all seemed to ride behind one another. Had they split up? Were we being misled?

I stopped and gave my nephew an ordered, "Conner, retrace the tracks back to the town's gate. But be careful."

We waited, but he soon caught us up. "Yes, they all came this way. Twelve all together, seven first, then five after trying to cover the first's tracks. Then five turned off. They tried covering their tracks, but they did not do a good job."

Hoping he was correct; we resumed our journey.

The weather held, so we made good time, but we still had at least two days' ride to the capital. That night, we camped close to the road and hid the fire in a freshly dug pit. Rylan cooked a wonderful stew and tea, which was more than welcome.

After we cleared up, Conner broached the subject of the missing blackbird, the head of our guild. Then we discussed the death of the head of the guild of merchants. And were they connected? I believed so. The crosses on the map were the homes of Guild Masters.

"Are the two boys, the 'from within' as stated in Philip's letter, or are we still looking for another?" I asked, though I expected no answer.

Conner reminded me of the possibility of three teachers, or could it be the horse master? He, too, was new to the post, and we often saw him talking to the boys. I thought on this and asked Rylan, "Was there anyone new that was engaged before your old master's son died?"

"Funny you speak of a horse master, for one was engaged to teach the son, not long after his third birthday. But he'd died of old age, when the boy was fifteen and they hired a new one to finish the boy's training. His name was Marsten and was a tall, dark-haired man and sullen, as though he hated the work. I caught him twice mistreating, not only the horses, but the boy too, and we had words. I planned to tell the Master the following day, but he was called away on business early the next morning. I was to ride and meet him at Somerland. However, I told him on our way back from the horse traders' show. The death had occurred while his father was away, where he bought the boy a new horse for his birthday, later that week. We arrived back to the devastating news and Marsten had gone. I wondered if he had something to do with it and the master's a few days later. I did not hold with it, as I said, and with the new master's death around thirty days later. I thought it was poison, but the doctor brought in by the magistrate said it was his heart. Could they both have died because they, whoever, wanted a new guild master, but if so, why take Philip Hakorn? Surely his son would become the owner of Hakorn if Philip dies, but who would be the new guild leader and the new head Blackbird? Master Philip was head of both, but that's a rear thing. I'm not a Blackbird, but I am a member of the warrior guild."

His assessment was quite good. I knew Drevis would know, but we would have to wait till we reached Lymol before we could find out. *Philip was the guild leader and the Blackbird, but who would be the next one, or two? Anslow was the next highest Blackbird, but the guild's captain, I wasn't sure.* Forty years of only being a member on parchment did not make me privy to inside information unless Philip asked something of me, though I recalled being given a roll call recently. A list of all the Blackbirds and guild members from Philip. I suddenly sat up, staring, and turned to Conner.

"What is it?" He asked, eyes wide open.

I told him, "Recently, I had sorted a list of members for Philip into areas, so that Blackbirds could be closer to their home territory, but also one assigned to a tower in case needed to be contacted by messenger bird urgently. Then he could ride to those in his territory. This would be quicker than sending a rider to each home. Philip had agreed, and it slowly was being implemented at last. In fact, I used for the first time yesterday it."

"And you have that list with you?" asked Rylan.

I shook my head. "No, a copy, but it's in my office at home."

Why I lied, I don't know. Conner knew too, for it was at his father's address in the safe. But I was uncertain at that moment who was trustworthy besides Conner. The original was with Philip, but where he kept it, I don't know. Was that what they wanted? Time would tell. At Lymol, I would send a message to Arthur, my nephew and warn him to check my office in my rooms every morning about a possible visitor. If he got a visit, I would know Rylan was the culprit. I would send a different message back to Hakorn and again time would tell. Greylan promised to recall the students and their teachers. I would see what version of my lie would come back to me. I settled down, no good worrying about it yet and I needed sleep.

By dawn, we were back on the road. We crossed the ford around midmorning and headed into the Ral Valley that would see us to the capital. It was getting cooler, and I was used to the southerly breezes of Pranda. I pulled my cloak closer to me.

By noon, we were ready for a break and we stopped by a stream to feed and water the six of us, but five men, who had other ideas, jumped out from the reeds in the water and ambushed us. We had kept eyes on both road and river, but not in the river, but we seemed to have had it under control, but help, no matter the form, was always welcome. Yet, I was unaware of any one following us until five people, one woman and four men, appeared out of nowhere. Their appearance startled me, giving my opponent time to strike, and I received a slash across my chest. I staggered back, but an elf dashed in and struck the man down.

I sat heavily on the ground as Conner dashed over. "Uncle?" He called, concerned.

I knew the wound was bleeding, but it wasn't deep, but I felt the warmth of the blood running down my chest. I pointed to my bag and Conner ran to it as the woman came over.

"Sorry," she said. She hesitantly tried to sit beside me, but Conner, seeing her struggle, helped, for which she thanked him.

"It's only a flesh wound," I informed her and the gathering crowd. "But tell me, my lady, what brings you here?"

"You know who I am?"

She did not recognise me, but then, it had been forty years. I nodded as I told her who I was. "I remember Michael's mother and his father." I told her, before I looked up at the elf standing near Kathryn, the Tralian Sorceress, and nodded a welcome. My Lord Macaith, and his cousin, Cadraith, who nodded back. And Prince Martin and Prince Jon, both I had recently met in Centra. Again, a nod from each of them. The four looked at their horses. As Rylan looked at ours.

"Well, First Minister, it's been a while?" Replied Kathryn with a smile.

"Aye, that it has, but welcome. I tried to take my pro-offered bag, but Kathryn waylaid it and reached in for a cloth to stem the bleeding, while I listened to her story.

"Two guild leaders have killed, and I was going to check on Phillip Hakorn when we heard this fight. We hurried here to see what it was and if we could help you. I'm sorry to have startled you."

"Hazards of fighting," I told her, dismissing the blame. "But your journey to Hakorn will be wasted. They took Philip, and we were following his abductors. There are at least five of them. Any alive that could talk?" I nodded to the dead.

I watched their reactions as I spoke. Kathryn's complexion whitened and the other four held a look of disbelief as they all shook their heads. I told her more.

"Pity. Ten days ago, I received a letter from Philip that brought me to Hakorn. There was an attempt to stop me from getting there. By bad luck, Rylan here was part of that attempt and did not take part when he saw how violent they were attacking our poor packs. Took my great nephew here almost two days to stitch up every hole. But good fortune for us as Rylan joined us and he's an excellent cook." I went on to tell her what he had told us, what Talaya had told us and the information from Marcus and what we believed.

As I spoke, a fire was lit for tea by the young prince. He seemed capable. The Elves searched the dead and then the others removed the bodies on the road, while the Sorceress and I drank our tea. The watch would be informed as soon as possible.

"Is this a new thing," she asked, "or a residue from my son's death?"

"As yet, uncertain." I replied.

She told me of the order of the golden snake and her clash with its leaders and how she was still looking for them and their box.

"And you say this box of power is what they want. Where do the guild heads come into this?" I asked.

"Sixty plus years ago, I fought Medrith, who had abducted the heirs to the four counties, including the elvish nation. He threatened to bury them alive if they did not crown him king. I saved the princes, but I wonder if killing the heads is the same thing. Medrith's heir, Wendle, wants the throne, so a change in leadership. But I will kill the heir to Medrith's madness and deprived the cult of the box, the first chance I get."

I nodded my head. "It sounds like they are trying to replace them with their own people, to what purpose has yet to be revealed. The heads are part of the king's council and one day a full council could be called and then they could influence the King to go their way for whatever reason in some power play of their own." I let her think of that before adding, "And what if they go further? Who's next, the Primes?"

"Impossible!" She declared hotly. "There are too many, but I get your meaning." She quickly cooled.

"If your nephew asked you where this box was, would you tell him?"

"He already knows of it, but we don't as yet know the location," she replied. But she understood his meaning.

"If your nephew, your great nephew or your great-great nephew was removed from the throne and they installed someone else, who would threaten the royal family, would you tell them if they asked?"

She thought for a moment, then nodded. "No, in case I had reason to believe they worked for the dark, or ill intentions to Tralia. I love my family dearly, but the Goddess placed a great trust in me to protect Tralia." She added sadly.

"Nevertheless, it is possible, and they would have their box back and the throne besides."

"Who would?" Ask Macaith as he sat down beside Kathryn. She told him about my scenario.

"That blasted box. Any chance we can destroy it?" He asked shortly.

"No, as we don't want to blow Tralia off the face of the map, but I will find a place they cannot reach it." She told him.

"Funny you should say map. That's what put us on the trail in the first place." Gregor told them.

I told her of Greylan's grandchildren.

"Blackbird fledglings, I don't believe it," said Martin, sitting down near his stepfather.

"Fraid' so," I responded. "Seems they have been disrupting the school for a few years and now were instrumental in opening the gates by killing the gateman. Greylan says he's washed his hands of them, yet Philip wrote that someone was trying to destroy the guilds from the inside. Two of the teachers are outstanding candidates as they are members of the Education Guild, not Blackbirds, but only Greylan is a Blackbird and I don't want to think it's a sworn member. They promoted Philip over his head ten years ago, as Greylan was ill. But I wonder if it is the warrior guild, they are trying to destroy. Though, it would have a deep impact on all the others if they do?"

"But where does that leave the other guilds?" Asked Conner.

"New heads have a new way of doing things," I replied. "But my primary concern is Philip. It seems he and I know something; and they want it. It cannot be this box of power, as I'm just hearing about it, so it can't be that. Then it has to be a list of all members that we recently drew up, organising the Blackbirds?" I explained a quick version of what Philip and I had been working on.

Kathryn nodded. "And controlling the King's council would be a good start to get that knowledge of the box." She pointed out. "And holding the rest of the council hostage would force mine, or the King's hand in making me tell where I will hide it, or to find it. And then there's this list. A powerful piece of information in its own right and a threat to kill each one on it."

"How many do they need to force the King's hand?" asked Cadraith.

I looked at the speaker, the cousin of Macaith, before I answered. "One dead to make the king sit up. An abduction would make him capitulate and three could make him abdicate." I looked at the Sorceress.

Kathryn agreed, "And he would order me to find or fetch it in two." She added again sadly.

I nodded too. "And as there are two deaths already, therefore, we have to find Philip in the next few days to prevent that scenario coming into fact."

"But where is he?" she asked.

I reached for the map and laid it on the ground between us. "If the black dots are the heads of fourteen guilds. Three now have red crosses through them. Orthney and Riverfalls we know about, but this one in Centra worries me. It the magic guild and there's been no attempt on the guild leader's life. and hopefully they can't get to the magic guild leader, but why is it crossed? Philip's has been taken, so there is the first of the two red circles, but this circle is Rivertown, what is its connection? No heads of guilds live there."

"That was a place used by Medrith, his daughter and his son's mercenaries. Could they be so stupid to use it again?"

"Possible, so it's where we are now heading. But I have also noticed. They hit Orthney first, then Riverfalls, then Hakorn. It seems they are moving south methodically."

I looked expectantly at the Sorceress. She tilted her head on one side before saying, "And if you're wrong?"

"I don't know, but as you can see, there is a cross through Orthney and that's head of the Education guild. Riverfalls was the Merchant Guild and three are already dead there. Therefore, who is the next target on their guild list? Centra? I have sent Blackbirds to the heads of the other guilds so hopefully; the enemy cannot get at them. And Rivertown is the only other circle along with Hakorn, what makes them different. Philip is the head of the warrior guild and the Blackbirds, but he was taken, not killed, why? Because of something he know?"

"I like your logic," said Macaith. "So, do we head south?" Though he looked at his wife, it was I who spoke.

"Yes!"

We headed to the ford, and crossed, before we camped for the night. We entered the town of Riverford a day later, just before dusk. The gateman nodded to us as we turned off the King's Highway and we made for the Riversedge inn.

Conner stated looking at the river "A boat down the Swain would be quicker." We agreed.

We ordered supper as Conner and the two elves went to find a suitable boat. They arrived back one bell later.

"One can take us to Lymol, but there we would have to find another as it was going east from there to Pranda."

My heart lurched. I did not want to go to Lymol. My inner voice cried, *the Blackbird whistled.* I nodded.

That night I dreamt again and Kiela answered. I slept till half bell to dawn and readied myself to go down stairs for breakfast. But my dream had puzzled me. Kiela had been weeping. Was it my dream or truth I did not know? But I held her in my arms for the first time in forty years.

Over breakfast, news of Philip's abduction had made the village. People were angry, especially after the recent death of the Tralian Ambassador.

"Why is it happening to this noble family?" They questioned. The watch had no answers.

We did not voice our thoughts. Conner and Martin headed into the market for fresh supplies and we were to meet them at the dock. They delayed the departure by half a bell to the captain's displeasure. I soothed him with a handful of extra coins and had to wait till we had got underway, before I got to them for their explanation.

Conner answered, "We were being followed, so Martin had the idea that we return to the market and circle around them. When they realised what we had done, they headed towards the dock. The two of us got in front and Martin spelled them as they came around the corner of a barn, where we were hiding. He questioned them. I had never seen a magic user draw out answers like that. It was fascinating."

I coughed.

"Sorry," he said before adding, "anyway, they told us Philip was at Rivertown, but they did not know in which part of the town. They do not know who the leaders are, only the leader of the five, their group. They had been waiting in the trees to watch as five other riders passed them, in case someone followed them. The others had travelled down river and would be there by now."

"Why?" Martin asked.

"A list of the Blackbirds that could stop them. There were twenty of them sent to Hakorn. It surprised them when they spotted you on the way there. They thought you had retired, so never considered your name would be on the list. They sent five to stop you, but two stayed in the trees and watched when you were attacked. This was a mistake."

"I knew nothing of others. They were not party to my group," interrupted Rylan.

"They did not trust the three sent after us," continued Conner, "so they followed and was reported back that they had failed to stop us. Their leader gave them a new assignment. They wanted more time at Hakorn, but our arrival there halted that, so they took Philip instead. When they reached Riverford, they split up. Five went by boat down the Swain with Philip and that left five to go up to Orthney to report, leaving two at Riverford to watch and try to stop you if you turned up. These two were to follow north after they attacked us and stopped us from getting on the barge. They also needed to find out what we were doing and who our new travel companions were. We asked where in Orthney was the others, but they bit into something in their mouths and they died quickly. Well, they won't be talking, ever!"

"They are looking for the list you have as they could not find it at Hakorn." Martin told them. "They know you have a copy. The two from the first five went to Pranda a week ago and searched your rooms and the first minister's office in Pranda, but a lad, who disappeared fast, had spotted them. So, they had to leave, but the Prime arrested them at the gate and were awaiting the king's justice in the watches dungeon when they killed themselves too."

"Sandras would have sent word to both Centra and Orthney." I told them. And was glad that Rylan hadn't told them. "They must have gone straight to Pranda they saw me?"

Kathryn agreed.

It took a few hours to travel past Centra and a few more to reach the Bridge at Lymol, where this boat ride finished. We called at The Riverside inn for a meal and to hear that there had been an attack on the head of the Magic Guild, and they had killed Chelseia. The news was awful.

Chapter Three
Old Wounds Closed

Kathryn, Macaith, and Martin vanished for a few hours as the rest of us kicked our heels. The next boat ride could not begin till dawn the next morning and we needed to brush the horses down. So, I went back with an elf, Rylan and Conner, to the livery and started on the task. Eight divided by four did not take long, and once outside, I decided on a walk.

Conner and Rylan were up for it, but Cadraith needed to get back to see if Macaith and Kathryn were back.

"Very well. We will be back for supper." He nodded and waved a hand as he departed.

For an hour, we walked through the town. Keeping close to the bridge. We saw many people of all different races and even a tall blond. I did not know where Kiela lived and I did not want to run into her and her husband, but he was a bargeman and could easily take the air after a day's work. Of all the places in Tralia, Lymol was by far the busiest.

It was the connection to anywhere, whether by boat or horse, as there were very few places to cross. The river Swain was the largest river in Tralia and separated east from west. Starting in the far north and ending in the southern sea. The Eastern River separated the north and the south. So, no matter where you wanted to go, Lymol crossroads was the best place to start.

It had a few taverns and if you needed a bed, a few inns. But it was too early to go to bed and Conner wasn't old enough to sit in a tavern or inn, though he looked older than he was. But I wanted a drink!

We went into a tavern's yard as it sat close to the river and we watched the traffic travel up and down the water. I ordered an ale and a half. The keep got the message, and it wasn't long before the drinks arrived. A full ale for me and a watered half for Conner. He took a sip and screwed up his nose.

"This is awful, Uncle. How can you drink it? The ale at Hakorn is much better."

I laughed. I had not thought that Philip served ale to the fledglings, but then water could be bad at anytime and anywhere. Though they had their own well. Many things I had not considered as I thought of Conner. I had set him on a path that could get him killed, but it kept him off the streets as most boys of seventeen were prone to do once their day's work had finished. This brought most under the eye of the watch, but I knew little about teenage boys. I had given my word to his father that while in my care I would watch over him. Yet, I did not believe he needed watching that closely. He had an aptitude that was worthy of a man, not of a child. He listened well in school and even to his father and elder cousin Thomas, who was his father's heir as Conner had been born well after his sisters. Good job too, as Conner did not like politics and loved his training at Hakorn. He would do well in the Castle Warriors. Both Thomas' uncle and myself trained Thomas, so he was a suitable heir and already completed almost seven years before Conner was born. Arthur agreed to his son joining the warrior guild. Sandras was also ready to retire and soon Gallard would take over from his father and become Prime of Pranda and he needed people he could trust. I had already spoken to Philip about Conner becoming Gallard's bodyguard after Conner finished his training at Hakorn, and he agreed that the man had potential. Luckily Gallard, Thomas and Conner like each other, and could work closely together as they had proved this last two years. Though Master Sharn was the bodyguard at present, but he too was ready to retire and could complete Conner's training, at least for the few years he had left and there was also Gallard's son to be considered. He too would need watching over. Master Sharn's own son was considered.

I hoped their friendships would grow through the years. Conner's cousin had already produced an heir, so staying in the warrior guild wouldn't be a problem for Conner and I have already set aside a stipend to see to his board and lodgings at the castle, as was the custom.

Conner recalled my attention to the river again by pointing to a small craft being rowed by a group of Lymols. They were practicing for the next boat race against Pranda. Pranda held the colours at the moment, but it passed it back and forth every other year. I watched as the boat turned to the landing, and it looked as though they were ready to come ashore. It was then I saw a man watching us from over on the other bank. Well, he was watching the Tavern, but we had cause to be watched. I moved my hands and Conner moved his. We drank up and went back to the road. We waited a few moments, then looked back to the opposite bank, but the watcher had gone.

The boatyard was near and a check up on other boats could not hurt, so we turned east and wandered down the road that led to the river's towpath. It wasn't dusk yet, and the walk was pleasant enough. We saw many boats of all different types, mostly working boats, by people earning a living from their homes.

My mind wandered again. *Could any of these barge men be Kiela's husband? Does he hold her at night when her fears come? Does he kiss her tenderly and…?* I shook the thoughts away as Conner was giving me a funny look.

"Problem uncle?"

"Nothing to bother yourself about. That boat three is like the one I'm buying. The one with the sails." I changed his focus.

"Truly; and will you invite me aboard?" He grinned.

"Of course, you can learn to sail her and then take over and sail or barge me around the harbour in my dotage." I laughed.

He shrugged, "Well, at least it will keep me from home."

"Problem nephew?" I asked, in the same tone he'd used before.

"Sisters," he replied. "Older, nosey, noisy sisters with babies. Crying babies." He added a little bitterly.

"Maybe now, but soon they will be a comfort and you never know, a great niece or nephew might turn out to be a goddess sent."

He thought for a moment, then his grin surpassed mine.

"Truly?"

I nodded. "My sister's grandchild was worthy of my time, but well, sorry, but I never took to your grandfather, but your father was worthy of my position and one day your cousin will be too.

But you, my lad, may just be a budding leader of the Blackbirds or the Captain of the Castle Warriors guild, maybe even guild leader."

"Again, Truly?"

Again, I nodded. Which brought us back to the task at hand.

"Do you think we'll find Master Philip?"

I nodded. "I hope so. He's more than 'The Blackbird' to me. He's my friend and hopefully by tomorrow night we'll have found him, but I won't lie. I'm worried. He's not a young man and, like myself, too old to be chasing around Tralia."

"But the Sorceress is older than both of you?" He pointed out.

I laughed. "Aye, she is, lad, but then she has magic. I don't."

"No, I guess you don't, yet I heard she travels by horse instead of using her magic."

"That's because she cares about her health and besides, she'd miss so much beauty if she just jumped everywhere!"

"I guess so," he agreed.

A boat went by, turning us back to the river because of the rushing sound. A rowing boat. We began walking again.

"I've been thinking, uncle, my two years are up by the end of the year and after the fire festival, will we still go to stay with the prime and his family in the country house?"

"Not for me, I'm sorry to say, that privilege goes to your father now, but like me, he may take you too."

He nodded and again I saw my sisters' eyes smiling back. *Isabel,* I thought, *you may have married a money grasping idiot, but your son and grandson turned out all right.*

At the end of the towpath, we saw the entrance to the boatyard and hurried to our destination in case they closed up at dusk. There were a few boats lined up, some needing repairs and others protection during the night, like the rowing boat being taking in. It would be stacked alongside others and chained to a sturdy metal post. The Lymols were just walking through the gates carrying their boat.

The first boat we looked at was only a small barge, but large enough to carry grain from the western fields to the northern docks. But it wasn't what I required. The second one looked interesting, but nothing I would choose. An attack vessel newly built by the looks of it and looked ready to join the fleet at Pranda and probably awaiting sailors to take it down the eastern river to its new home in the harbour. Prandains make splendid sailors, but Lymols were the boat builders and had been for thousands of years. Yet this boatyard was owned by a human, by the name of the gate. Unusual as Lymols own all the yards in Lymol. This man must have earned a name for himself.

I heard a door open and close somewhere behind me, but I continued telling Conner about the attack vessel before us when I heard my name whispered. I knew the voice and knew my life would change if, when I turned around, as I knew I had to.

"Kiela!" I said, looking at the tall woman with long blond-white hair tied up into a pile on the top of her head. A soft complexion was now lined as age gets to us all eventually, but her summer blue eyes were the same, yet they seemed red from weeping. "It's been a long time?" I said.

"Too long," she replied. "I have seen the others many times, but not you. Your prime said you were busy each time when he came to Centra. I got the impression you were avoiding me."

I shook my head. "Always busy," I said, "but now I'm retired and soon I'll have more time on my hands than I know what to do with."

"Is that why you're looking at boats, though I would not think an attack vessel was your type, a barge maybe?" She enquired.

"Aye, a barge maybe, but more a sailboat. There's one already with my name on it, but I have something to do before I can go boating."

"Really, your prime hasn't let you retire just yet, then?" She laughed.

A sound my heart remembered, and it made a double beat. Conner had moved off to look at another boat.

"No, not my prime. My friend Philip Hakorn has gone missing."

"Talaya's brother?" She sobered at my words. "She doesn't need more heartache, what with Michael and all?"

I nodded my agreement.

"And the Sorceress, what she is doing, though another heartache, I don't think she can handle either?"

"Tougher than most people think." I said, knowing my assessment of Kathryn was correct.

"Possibly, but from what I hear, losing her son has done much damage to the King's family?"

"That's true, but she's here with me, looking for Phillip."

"Well, it doesn't surprise me, but why here?"

"We're travelling down to Rivertown. It's quicker than riding, but we can't leave till dawn."

"And you, have you done much boating?"

"My Prime's brother-in-law has taught me much over the years."

"You never married?" She asked bluntly, but I think she already knew my answer. I shook my head.

"I was," she said, causing another heart to flutter. "But he died four years ago."

A bigger flutter. "And my eldest son followed his father, a tenday ago."

"And you were crying recently because of it?"

She nodded. "Walk with me and I'll show you the rest of the yard. I feel I owe you an apology for the way I treated…"

I stopped her with a hand in the air. "No, I just thought if I pressed my case, you might have changed your mind."

"I wouldn't have, as I had already given my word before we met and Delor had to keep face as our father was dead. There was nothing I could do. But he was a good man, and he left my son this, on the proviso that he let me live in the boathouse."

Her arm waves to include the yard and the house behind her until she stopped, "But he's dead. The yard goes to my husband's cousin as I did not bear another son. I have two daughters and they are both married with families of their own and now my husband's cousin wants the house for him and his new wife."

"When do you have to move out?"

"Within ten days. If things had been different, I hoped I would be looking with you at your boat. I often dreamed of a life with you." I stepped forward as she brought her hands to her face.

I stopped her tears by saying, "There's no reason you cannot now. You are free to marry again, so will you?"

"Are you asking, even after forty years of change?"

"You don't look that different, except possibly more beautiful." I opened my arms, and she stepped into them.

"It's been too long," she said. I agreed.

"But I need to find Philip before I can go boating. Will you wait?" She nodded.

"If you need to stay anywhere, I will find you, or go to my old office at Pranda castle and my nephew will make the arrangements. I will give you a letter to give to him."

She nodded again as a small smile crossed her lips and I took advantage. But then stepped back and grinned, "I should not put ideas into the lad's head."

I turned my head and looked for Conner, but I could not see him, instead I saw two men deep in conversation standing near the gate. I pulled Kiela to one side, then sent her inside as I continued to watch.

****

Conner

Conner had seen them and watched the two together and knew they had history.

Their conversation was not for my ears, he thought, *they weren't exactly arguing, but there was some displeasure. Raised voices always make me look.*

They turned and walked away, back towards the town. As he wandered down the row of boats, his mind was on the two that had been watching and what of the other, the one on the other side of the river? Where was he now? He wondered who he was and was he part of the abductors? It seemed possible. Conner knew he wasn't strong enough to take him on. He had looked well-built and definitely wore a sword, but if we knew where he was, we could follow? How many inns and taverns did this place have? *Was he staying nearby?* he thought. It was not a place Conner knew, as he had only been two or three times in his life. His mind wandered to Master Philip, and he knew whoever had taken him wasn't fooling around. They wanted something. Could it be the box of power the Sorceress talked about? We needed Master Philip back, but we could not exchange him for this box, if it was as dangerous or as powerful as made out.

Conner walked on, looking at the boats, yet not really seeing them. But he was watchful and saw a movement at the other end of the boat that he now stood in front of. If he had run, he may have caught whoever was there, but he was not a man of foolish thinking or actions, as he had been told on more than one occasion. So, Conner moved on and, as he did, he released the leather strap on the hilt of his sword. By now the boat's hull fully hid him. Conner hurried back the way he'd come and then down between the two boats he'd just passed. At the far end, he stopped and peered around the corner. There stood a man, who was looking down the alley Conner would have taken. Not the watcher from previously and not the two who had stood outside the gate, either. Lucky for him, this man was around his own size.

Conner stepped forward and reached out. Conner poked the other in the back and stepped back as the other turned, noting the weapons that the other carried. Apart from the sword he held, he had a blade tucked into his belt. Maybe a couple of blades in his black knee-length boots. All could cause damage. *Do not get too close to your quarry and do not grip the sword too tight,* ran through Conner's mind. The memory from the first week of training. All actions could cause them to take you down or break your wrist. The man had dark hair and a grim mouth, and the look of surprise that changed to a look of pure hatred in his dark eyes. Yet Conner did not know him, so why the look? *He'll tell me,* the younger man thought. He watched as the other drew his sword, but by his stance Conner knew he was a soldier, not a warrior. They had taught him the difference in his first year at the age of seven. The man stepped forward and his sword rose. Conner blocked it easily and asked, "Where's Philip Hakorn?"

The man faltered with both the repercussion of the sword and Conner's words. He rallied and tried to strike again. "Somewhere you can't find him; and when he tells my master what he needs to know, then he'll die."

"And what is it that your master needs to know?" Conner asked.

He jumped back with a strange look in his eyes. "You'll find out!"

Conner thrust out sharply, cutting deep into the other's sword arm, but he held onto his weapon, much to the chagrin of Conner. Conner struck again. This time he caught the man's hand and with the blood dripping down his arm, the sword dropped to the ground, as the hilt became too slippery to hold. Not done yet, the soldier pulled a knife from his belt with his other.

So, he wasn't quite ready to give up just yet. "Why the hate?" Conner asked, just before he sucked in a deep breath as the other lunged.

"You Tralians are weak." The man spat out with venom, before he sneered.

"Really, but I'm not the one who's bleeding," Conner countered. "You Tralians? Where are you from then?"

"Further than you know," he laughed harshly.

"Hmmm," Conner thought before he replied. "A mercenary from Raabaal then." He announced sharply, knowing his history of the mercenaries as he lunged again, and again there was another surprise in his opponent's eyes.

"You know your leader will be dead soon, don't you?"

"You think you know everything. That puny sorcerer is not my master. My master is coming for you all and you won't see it coming."

"So, it's not yet, then?" Conner asked sarcastically.

"When he's ready, he'll come and only the sister will be here then. Only her loyal followers will be here. You'll all be gone. You twisted her teachings, then abandoned her. Her mother nor her sister, are as strong as the Goddess of the snake and soon there will be none who will oppose her or my master. All will be gone, just like you!" He struck out and his knife, making a scratch on Conner's middle finger.

"This conversation is getting old too quick. I'll let My Master question you." Conner stated, emphasising the two words, but to his surprise the man grinned, just before he drew the blade across his own throat and that's when Conner saw his uncle step out. Shocked, Conner turned with his bloody blade pointing at him, as for a moment the man did not register. Conner raised it to strike to defend himself, but a woman screamed, and they heard a lot of running footsteps before he turned and vomited his lunch.

"Conner, what in the Goddess' name has happened? Please tell me you did not…"

"What, no!" he interrupted. "Goddess no. He did it to himself as I was about to take him prisoner." It surprised Conner to think he could think so. But then who would think a man would cut his own throat? There was something about his grin that worried him as well as this strange feeling soaring through him. "Uncle, did the history of the Blackcoats tell of poisonous blades?" Conner asked, as he looked at the wound on his right middle finger.

"Some, why are you… Conner!"

The darkness came. Gregor watched his nephew fall to the ground beside the dead man.

Chapter Four
A Diversion

I watched, as one rower we saw earlier carry Conner to Kiela's house and laid the boy down on her bed. I did not have time for the thought that flipped across my mind as I waited for a second rower to fetch a healer and a third ran to the Riversedge to see if Kathryn was back. This was not how I imagined the boy would die, but without knowing what poison was on the blade, how could he not? Kiela did the best she could with the few herbs she had.

"A wife and mother pick up a few things along the way," she said, for something to say, "but I am no healer."

The healer came within the quarter bell, as he only lived a few roads away. But it was almost a bell before Kathryn and the others got here, as the rower had to wait. She smelt the blade and set to work, magic and herbs, but the worst part was the not knowing and waiting.

I told the elves and Rylan what had happened and about being watched. Cadraith wanted a description, and I gave one. He and Macaith left shortly after, and so had Rylan, and none said why. I sat by the bed for the rest of the night.

Dawn came and went and there was no sign of him waking up, but there was also no sign he was getting any worse, so maybe that was a good thing.

"I expected his fever to come," the Sorceress stated. "But he has none." She seemed pleased with his progress.

Kathryn sat in a chair on the other side of the bed and rested her arms on the bed and dozed.

Kiela was busy packing, but from what I saw her husband had left little and the boatyard, that was worth anything was going to an obnoxious cousin. Three boxes and a few cloth bags. I noticed as I stretched my legs. One cart would see her to Pranda. Well, it did not matter. Soon she'd want for nothing.

Noon came and went, and the plate of food sat on the dresser, but the water pitcher was empty and gone. Kiela had taken it to refill. The watch came and left, promising to watch out for any black dressed men in town. The elves had not returned. But Rylan had, but left again soon after. He had been and fetched our things from Riversedge, now he had gone to the market as there was little food here. The daughters had given what they could, with their husband's blessing, but the cousin refused to help. All payments were now made to him from the boat yard and he cared naught for Kiela welfare, whether or not she starved.

The boat we had hired had left at dawn, but boats came and went during the day and would continue to do so. Kathryn told the king about Philip and he sent a few men to watch Rivertown. A few Blackbirds had heard about Conner and found their way here and some were watching the house and others, the town. Two fledglings also had heard about Conner, their friend. so, are now seconded in the yard, swords ready.

The enemy could watch, laughing at the diversion or could move Philip in case their man had talked. I went down into the yard and paced, torn between my nephew and my friend. I thought about what I knew. Was Kathryn correct? Was it the box they wanted? Yet no one it seems knows where it is. But I needed more information, however I knew Kathryn would not tell me where she thought the box was and to be truthful, I did not need to know. The box to me wasn't important, I needed to know more about these mercenaries, so I could find them. I went back upstairs to ask questions, but the answers weren't helpful.

The Sorceress explained, "They came from over the mountains. From the old world, Raabaal. They worshipped the sister of our Goddess, but she disobeyed the mother and the father made her lover disappear. She is searching for him. The Blackcoats enslaved many, especially young girls to breed from. An army was bred, but a year ago their enemy decimated them as the Tralian army was trained well. Unlike the master who did not teach them, not even basic sword play. They chopped at their opponents, or attacked with a knife, just like with Conner, but to dip a blade into poison that was bad, but it was known."

He nodded his thanks when she finished speaking.

"You forgot something," said Conner, opening his eyes. "Their leaders don't leave Raabaal."

He looked younger than he usually did. A vulnerability I hadn't seen before, one he had never shown.

"Not unless they have to. I heard about one and he hates women, or at least they treat them no better than cattle. Though the world is changing, and men are thinking differently about women, there are still those who think we are nothing more than slaves to serve their purposes." Kathryn gave a terse nod to the men that surrounded her.

"I know," said the youth, "but the more we teach the young ones, the more that attitude will dissipate."

"Correct. Teaching is the best approach," replied Kathryn. "I'm glad you're feeling better."

"Thank you. I am, but we missed the boat," he added when he realised the time. "I'm sorry."

Kathryn tutted. "We could not travel without you," she smiled, "and you need to recover."

I agreed, patting his arm.

"Well, I'll recover enough to travel by boat tomorrow."

"We'll see," she stated firmly.

I nodded again, when he looked at me.

He capitulated and closed his eyes and went back to sleep.

Later that afternoon in the kitchen, the elves who had returned told us about the discussion they had with my watcher. They found him in a livery putting a saddle on a black horse that seems wasn't his, but before they called the watch, they questioned him elfin style.

"As far as he knew, Philip was still at Rivertown, but his master could have moved him by now. They are after the box as it holds great power and only a staunch believer can use it. They won't give up. No, they weren't sorcerers, but he knew a sorcerer could use it to enhance his ability. His masters where once known as shadows and lived a long time, but not since a man called Horold stole the box. It happened a long time ago and was kept by his family, which helped them to live longer, but unlike his masters it sent them crazy. He added, 'They believed that the power was a gift from the elder sister. All men once worshipped her, until the mother came along, then the Tralian worshipped her and the second daughter. This angered the eldest child, and she created a box to store her anger. When it was full, she would visit that anger upon her mother and sister. But the power kept being used by the shadow masters, so it would never stay full. So, she arranged for it to be stolen. The sorcerers who stole it, realised it enhanced their power, but they misused it, and she took it from them too, but it's now lost, so she cannot fill it. I have been ordered by the Master, who is atoning for his sins to find it by any means possible and wipe out the leaders of the enemy also by any means necessary.' Then he slit his own throat."

"Fanatics!" exclaimed Jon, who had arrived in the afternoon. "Do you think we have to go to Raabaal again?"

"We can only determine that once we have been to Rivertown," put in Kathryn. "But we may one day have to remove the masters once and for all. Or at least I will."

That evening, Kiela and I went for a walk. I had written two letters for her and she now held them in her left hand, the other hand I held in my own. We had an escort, one fledgling, Timus, on instructions from Conner, who was already up and about, though confined to the house and yard. I told Conner about how we met that afternoon and he had kindly written to his father on her behalf, though what he actually put was unknown. They seemed to get on well. When we got back, Master Conwell, the husband's cousin, was waiting to speak to Kiela. I stood to one side, but close if he upset her.

"Ten days," He said. He was loud and obnoxious. "That will be up tomorrow, and I did not say you could let out any rooms."

I had heard enough, but before I spoke, Conner stepped out into the yard. "That will do," he said with authority. "The only reason you want her out is because you have sold it, against your cousin's wishes and the will states you should find a suitable premise for your cousin's wife if you want to live on the premises."

Kiela looked stunned. I wondered how he knew, but then he had spoken to both fledglings that afternoon. Either they knew or one had gone and asked questions. Blackbirds were good at gathering information.

"What has this to do with you?" The man said gruffly.

"A lot. My father is the Prime of Pranda's first minister and my mother is the daughter of the first minister of the Prime of Centra, a dear friend of Kathryn, the Sorceress of Tralia. So, if you don't want any of them to know how you have treated my great aunt-to-be, I suggest you start by talking civilly to her as Kathryn is here."

"Someone called?" said the lady in question as she stepped into the yard.

"Nothing I can't deal with, my lady." He bowed, then turned back to the cousin. "Isn't that correct, Master Conwell?" he emphasised the last two words.

The man had visibly whitened as Conner had spoken and with the arrival of Kathryn, well, the white now looked positively grey.

"Yes, I… I will see to new premises straight away." Fear took ahold of the shock as he looked at Kathryn.

"No, what you will do is escort my great aunt-to-be, to my father's house in Pranda where she will stay till her forthcoming marriage to my uncle, while we are away on business. If I hear of any misstep, you will have to answer to me. Got it!" Conner had taken a few steps closer and was holding the hilt that was still sheathed, but he loosened the leather strap for further impact.

"No misstep, I can assure you. Of course, it will be my duty and pleasure," he added quickly before continuing, "as the head of the family to see her safely to Pranda," he added quickly. "When will this journey start?"

Conner looked at Kiela, "When the Mistress is ready and not a bell before. Do I make myself clear?"

"Of course, I will do as you say." He too looked at Kiela. "Please, Mistress Keila, inform me when you are ready."

She nodded; the colour soon returned to her cheeks. I stepped closer and took her hand as the cousin bowed and turned away.

"Make it soon, Kiela." I stated, not liking the fellow to keep his word. She nodded.

"Don't worry," Conner told us, "The two fledglings will also escort you and see to nightly lodgings along the way. Will you see to payment uncle…" he turned to me, "or," he grinned, "should I make the cousin pay?"

Laughter broke the tension in the air. Conner was back.

"What a nasty little fellow to be sure," put in Kathryn before turning. She re-entered the house. We followed. "Should I spell the house to have a ghost as punishment?" She murmured.

"At least two," put on Conner. "He deserves at least two."

We laughed again, just as the elves got back from arranging our passage down river. Kathryn filled them in.

We all sat around Kiela's dining table after supper and Kathryn told us about Chelseia, the head of the magic guild.

"The rumours were partly true, but she isn't dead. Her second had arrived just in time to prevent her from drinking poison when he asked which vineyard the wine bottle she was holding had come from. He overlooked all wine deliveries and did not recall from where it came. They put it out she died to flush out the culprits, but no one has stepped forward and owned up. Then they said the rumours were false, she was fine." The Sorceress gathered her thoughts before she continued. Obviously she knew the other Sorceress well.

"And..." stated Kathryn, "they won't do. These Masters hide, while their slaves do their dirty work, but I'm sure there were five of them, brothers, I believe, but three died recently. My son spoke of one he saw, and he was ancient. He obviously used the power from the box and kept himself alive

I saw Martin flinch, so he they had an inkling where it was, but we both kept quiet.

"So, we leave before dawn?" asked her husband.

We agreed and by ten bells, most were asleep. A d two were on watch. Kiela had her bed back and Kathryn and Macaith had the guest room. The rest of us slept in the living, dining room and the kitchen. I had the living room and the hard-wooden sofa as Conner had the floor. He had the better option, though he disagreed. I was still awake when the church bells rang midnight and I also heard breaking glass. I nudged Conner awake and he and I softly edged our way to the door. But we need not have worried. Both fledglings had earned their wings, for in the kitchen they captured two men. The first thing Conner did was search them for weapons and not just the ones in their belts. Keila did not need to be cleaning up blood off her kitchen floor. The elves, Jon and Rylan, piled into the small room not moments later. The first two slipped out the front door, while Conner and Rylan went out the back.

Kathryn walked in and, though she looked tired, she got to work. Timus had already asked who they were.

"They laughed and said they would not be answering questions, but it was enough for Kathryn to enter one of their minds."

"What are you here for? She asked them. They did not even look at her as they didn't recognise a woman as someone worth speaking to, but she got her answer. They looked at me."

"They came to kill the First Minister?" Kathryn spoke aloud. Shock registered. "Apparently, they had not been told that Kathryn was a sorcerer, or they did not know she was here?" I moved my hands. She nodded. "Well, what am I going to do with you now?"

But Conner had not been as thorough as he thought. Both the men sneered, before biting down hard. I could do nothing as we watched the two men die. No blood, but poison!

At the sound of four bells, we were all gathered in the kitchen again. Kiela produced an excellent breakfast and then the two of us left to say our goodbyes.

"If this wasn't so important." She hushed me.

"Go find Philip. He's important." She told me. "I'll be safe enough. The fledglings cannot be bought, and the Blackbirds are around too. So, will see me right. Therefore, calm your mind, beloved. We will soon be together again."

The kiss made me want more, and my heart ached as we separated. "I cannot give a time, my love, but as soon as I can, I promise." Though tearful, she nodded.

"Soon." She repeated. The bells of five soon rang out and by half past, we were ready to leave.

I picked up my pack, and we set off to the jetty. Kiela waved and my heart lurched, but we would see each other and not long after we would be married. I asked Conner's father to place the banns for us and as we needed no one's permission, the priest would read them out on the first church service. The two tendays would fly by.

The walk by the river was what I needed, but the morning chill was still heavy, and the path was misty in places but the sun tried hard to shine between the clouds. Kathryn walked her husband as Cadraith walked with Martin, while Jon and Rylan walked in front and Conner and I brought up the rear.

The walk was uneventful, unless the walk along the river itself was an event. Birds tweeted as the sun popped up over the trees and at time shimmered on the water. Animals skittered away as we got close rustling through the underbrush. A pleasure to be sure as Kathryn puts it, but we did not stop, so we arrived at the barge in good time. I sat with the Sorceress as the others saw to storing the packs while others went for the horses. Soon we would be off.

Chapter Five
A Disused Fear

Conner had our horses and Martin held Kathryn's and Macaith's, while Jon and Rylan had the other three and they were now safely on board the large barge. Macaith helped his wife on board and Cadraith and I was the last to board. We took them in case we needed them, and we now did not have time to purchase or find more if we needed to travel inland and fast. The barge was large enough to take the eight of us, a captain and four crew and the animals. It also carried a hundred sacks of grain. The King's Messenger, it was called and its Captain, who was a stout fellow, said he knew the Swain like the back of his hand, started down the river. The rivers momentum carried the boat and the sailors just kept it away from the banks.

We watched the bank for any hostility towards us, but unlike the river, both sides were quiet. Kathryn was sitting on a pillow provided by the captain saying, "It isn't right that a lady should sit on the floor."

Both Kathryn and her husband thanked him. I don't think he knew who she was.

Conner and Rylan seemed restless and paced the small space allotted to us, but the elves did not. They too sat on the floor on the other side of Kathryn, while I, Jon and Martin sat facing them to even out the weight. Each side was watching the opposite bank and so far, it was quiet.

Finally, Kathryn asked the two pacers to sit as they were a distraction from watching the countryside go by. They obeyed, and each took a seat either beside me or beside Kathryn. Soon Conner and the Sorceress were deep in conversation about people they knew, yet till now these two had never met. Kathryn had only corresponded with Conner's mother after she left Centra and Conner was away at Hakorn when Kathryn had visited Pranda on a stately visit.

I had the honour of escorting her and her husband around, while the king was in conference with Sandras. Kathryn expressed a desire to visit Mary, my niece-in-law and her mother who was also on a visit to her daughter's, but that was a few years ago. I liked Mary when I had visited the first Minister of Centra and his family and introduced her to my nephew. He took the hint as she was more than worthy and luckily, he thought so too, but I left it to their fathers to talk terms. Her dowry was a good size and helped her husband to grow his fortune. I kept my watch, and the journey continued.

We arrived later that day and it took almost two bells to get off the barge. Our group turned away from the smell and headed back to the gatehouse and it was behind the grey box that we stopped.

We camped beside the river that night, just outside of Rivertown. Within the hour, a few blackbirds joined us and we scouted the town and scoured the trees. It was a small town, but by the smell of it, you would think it was a city like Pranda. Yet it was busier than most of the towns and villages on the Swain. We came upon a small group about to eat supper. We knew they were mercenaries; just not sure if they were a part of the snake's group. Conner stepped forward, and we were sure then as the group wasn't interested in talking to a stranger and one cock sure of himself, drew his sword.

The fighting started just as we entered the edge of the Somerland trees. I left the Blackbirds to deal with the mercenaries. After Conner had killed his man, I held him back.

"Time enough for you to spill blood again," I whispered.

Though disappointed, he obeyed. I called the town's fledglings and told them to follow the elves and we skirted the fighting. The older blackbirds had this well in hand and would follow as soon as they had finished here. We headed to the King's Highway, crossed and then on into the town meeting no resistance.

We entered Rivertown at dusk. I instructed the gate keep, "Keep quiet of our arrival. There will be more Blackbirds flying in."

He had nodded and gave some unexpected information concerning an old disused brothel on the northern edge of town near the river and a few unknowns within.

"For the past week, someone has used it." He added.

I thanked him and told it could be useful. We left the horses at the nearest stable and made the rest of our way through the town on foot. It was now dark and each wearing a black cloak, we slipped through easily. There were few about, some in the inns and taverns, others had finished work and were home putting their feet up, no doubt.

I glanced back and instructed those behind us, "Fan out and approach from all angles."

No questions were asked before the Blackbirds and fledglings obeyed. One had stayed near the gate to inform the others where we had gone. He was also a healer, so could tend to the injured, if needed. We travelled the streets till we came to the corner if the street where the brothel was situated and peering down, we saw the aforementioned building. The one next to last on the left-hand side. The moon had sailed up to almost its zenith before disappearing behind a cloud, throwing us all into total blackness. That's when I saw the small chunks of light.

By midnight, all were in place. One final whistle and we pushed forward. All windows and doors were covered. We entered, and I went in through the front door that fell off its hinges by the merest touch. Conner and I caught it before it made any noise. We left it leaning up against the wall, out of the way. I felt a cold sweep into my body and turned to Kathryn.

"A residue of power," she told me. "I have already dealt with it."

I shrugged, but the feeling I got that whatever it was, I did not think it was completely gone. I moved forward slowly. Some stairs went up and a few blackbirds flew off in that direction. The Sorceress of Tralia and her husband seemed to know where they were going, so I followed. They headed into a makeshift kitchen, that was empty, then through a door and inside were more stairs that descended. So did the four behind Conner and I, while six of the Blackbirds separated and searched the rest of the ground floor. We heard fighting mostly lasting only a few moments, but only true swordsmen lasted longer, and these weren't swordsmen.

Kathryn believed these were slaves that were dragged into an army and their training was poor at best, but their leader taught them from an early age that if caught, kill yourselves. A few of the mercenaries could be from the army that had fought a year ago and could be the teachers now. It was possible, but I did not want to go to Raabaal to find out. Downstairs, there was a corridor with doors on either side. Inside one, we found our Blackbird.

They had tied him to a chair, and he looked up. He had a black eye and a cut cheek. Blood dribbled from his mouth. Kathryn did as much as she could, but it seemed weird that Philip tried to stop her.

He mumbled, "It's a trifle nothing to worry about and now that I am free, I can heal faster. They are after the Orthney prince. We must stop them."

Kathryn closed her eyes.

"The Masters were gone, leaving only a few slaves to watch over Master Philip." Said one Blackbird. "They must have got wind of us closing in and did a moonlight flit." The Blackbirds searched, but there were no masters. Someone joked they had slithered underground. Kathryn was thoughtful after she opened her eyes and with their pale skins, the joker may not be far wrong. Yet, the entrance was not to be found either.

It took two bells to have Philip home, thanks to Martin. Then after he had taken Kathryn and Philip and his granddaughter and his sister whisked him into bed in moments. He came back for us. I don't think I care for magic travel and asked how he was, resting I was told, so I left him to sleep. I went back into the yard where Kathryn was saying her goodbyes. I thanked her for her help.

"All in a day's work," she said, turning to her husband, "and there were plenty more days like this one in front of them. They were off to find Medrith's son."

Their horses were ready to take them to Centra and back home and then they all vanished, though out of the gate. I too went for a nap.

Later I looked in to find Philip awake. "How you are feeling?" I asked, but he did not reply to my concern, instead he apologised for bringing me away from my first day of retirement.

"When the Blackbird whistles," I said, tilting my head.

"Aye, when the Blackbird whistles," repeated Philip as his eyes closed.

I closed the door as quietly as I could. There was nothing more to be done. He needed to rest to recover.

Now, I could go home. The following morning Conner and I were ready. But a dove arrived, and I waited in case it was news. It was, they had caught ten men including two fledglings who were screaming blue murder and wanted their grandfather. They would stand trial with their friends. The Prime's son was safe, thanks to Kathryn's warning and none had committed suicide.

Outside, Greylan asked if I knew they had caught his grandsons. I nodded my head. "I'm sorry, but they will always be scapegoats and their masters will appear again someday." I told him.

He agreed. "Like the proverbial bad penny," he added.

I nodded.

"I think Rylan would make a fine addition to the school." He told me after I had asked if the man could stay. He had proved his worth.

Rylan too thought so: a cook, a waiter and a swordsman, a fine combination. I laughed as I climbed into the saddle. With most of the fledglings back and a good portion of Blackbirds. I had no problems leaving my friends.

We stopped in Chaysford, to find the boat seller and pick up the documents of sale for my new vessel. I was happy to be going home. Conner was too. They gave him dispensation for not being in class for the next ten days as long as he was back shortly after to complete his training.

Epilogue

What an exhausting, yet exhilarating day to be sure. I had tied up the boat, 'No More Adventures,' up in a berth close to the Prandain harbour. The Sunset inn had one place to spare. I could finally climb into bed. Clem was asleep on his bed close by and had taken to his new mistress and would not leave her side. This time, I don't need to dream; my wife was already here.

I could see her blond-white hair popping out of the orange-coloured sheet as I settled in the chair to finally kicked off my shoes. and wondered on the perfection of it all. I could hardly believe my luck, but then I had waited a long time for lady luck to smile on me. I closed my eyes.

A bang abruptly awoke me and I opened a lazy eye to find Kiela sitting up in bed across the cabin, looking surprised and her shoe lying at my feet.

"You've moaned for forty years and now I'm here, you sleep in a chair." She said through gritted teeth in an angry whisper.

A smile emerged on my face as I shakily got up. "I was waiting for the next adventure," I replied, trying not to laugh. The smile grew on her face into a splitting grin.

"Well, it's not going to happen in that chair, is it?" She laughed.

I agreed as I slipped beneath the sheet. She giggled just like she had forty years ago, and the years slipped away as I finally held her in my arms.

The Characters of Tralia

Gregor: The newly retired First Minister of Pranda
Clem: Gregor's dog
Sandras: The Prime of Pranda
Quickfeet: A missive runner at Castle Pranda
Philip: Lord of Hakorn
Cecil: A castle cook at Pranda
Conner: Gregor's great nephew
Arthur: Gregor's nephew
Thomas: Arthur's nephew and heir to the first Minister
Michael: The late Ambassador of Tralia
Kathryn: The Tralian Sorcerer
Macaith: Kathryn's husband
Tilda: The Sorcerer's daughter. An abductor of
Kathryn's children forty years ago, who later died.
Medrith: The late sorcerer, who wanted to rule Tralia
Martin: Kathryn's adopted son
Jon Prince of Centra. Kathryn's Great-grand nephew
Rylan: A would be assassin, turned companion of
Gregor and Conner
Cadraith: Cousin of Macaith
Drevis: Hakorn's clerk
Talaya: Michael's wife and Philip's sister, who now
lives at Hakorn
Greylan: An old master, who lives at Hakorn
Marcus: Greylan youngest grandson
Jayson: Greylan grandson
Bradshaw: Greylan grandson
Chellin: A Teacher at Hakorn
Cordon: A Teacher at Hakorn
Brodel: A Teacher at Hakorn
Zarendrith: The Elfin stealth and hand-speak teacher
Kiela: Michael's blacksmith's friend's sister and
Gregory's only love
Conwell: Kiela's late husband's cousin
Timus: A fledgling at Lymol
Finley: A fledgling at Lymol

<u>Place Names</u>

<u>Castle Centra</u>- the Castle of the King of Tralia
<u>Centra Tunnels</u>-Beneath the castle at Centra
<u>Centra</u>-The town in which the King resides
<u>Ral Printer</u>-Village north of Centra close to Ral Valley
<u>The Riverboat</u>-An Inn in Ral Printer
<u>The Green</u>-An Inn in Ral Printer
<u>The Ford</u>-An inn in Old Riverford
<u>Orthney</u>-The Northern Capital
<u>Hakorn</u>-A farm manor and School for primes to be and princes. Philip's home
<u>Pranda</u>-The Eastern Capital
<u>Westlake</u>-The Western capital
<u>Rivertown</u>-A South Town on the River Swain
<u>Riversedge</u>-Inn in Westlake
<u>Esmud</u>-Oldest inhabited town in Tralia
<u>Tralia Town</u>-Old uninhabited town in the farthest north of Tralia
<u>Raabaal</u>-The original land of the Tralians

ABOUT THE AUTHOR

Thank you for choosing this book. If you enjoyed it, please consider telling your friends or leaving a review on Amazon, Goodreads or the site where you bought it. Word of mouth is an author's best friend and much appreciated.

Anita K Mills.

Follow her at: https://www.facebook.com/anita.mills.33

Website: https://blakemanbooks.weebly.com

YouTube https://YouTube.be/F4KtPER25oQ

OTHER BOOKS BY AUTHOR

<u>The Chronicles of Tralia</u>
Book 1: The Sorceress of the Five Crowns
Book 2: The Sorcerer's Daughter
Book 3: The Ambassador's Death

<u>A Debutant's Mystery</u>
Book 1: Beckett's Treasure
Book 2: Victoria's Nightmare

<u>The Tales of Tralia</u>
Book 1: When The Blackbird Whistles

Fibromyalgia: What a Pain